Too Many Time Machines

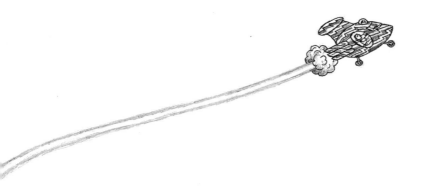

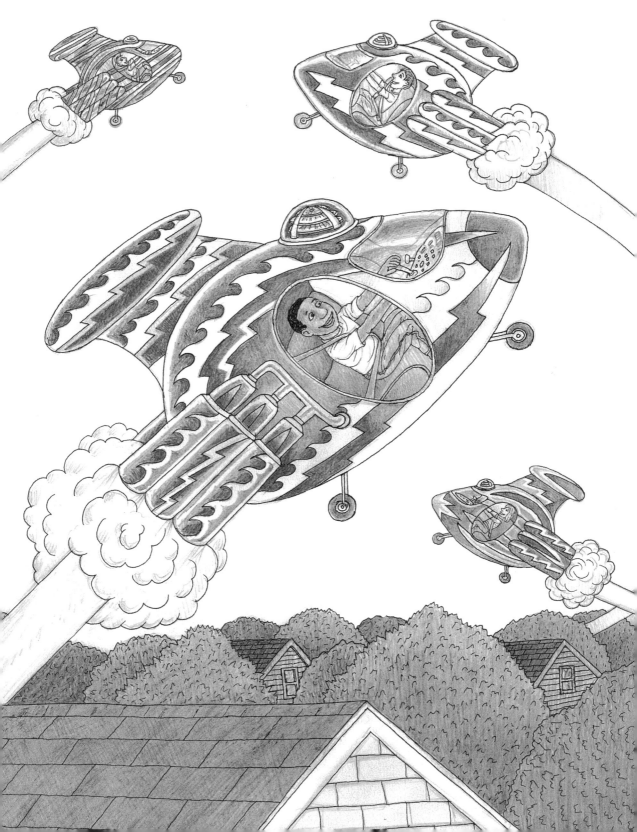

TOO MANY TIME MACHINES

or, The Incredible Story of How
I Went Back in Time, Met Babe Ruth,
and Discovered the Secret of Home Run Hitting

MARK ALAN STAMATY

VIKING

VIKING
Published by the Penguin Group
Penguin Putnam Books for Young Readers, 345 Hudson Street, New York, New York 10014, U.S.A.
Penguin Books Ltd, 27 Wrights Lane, London W8 5TZ, England
Penguin Books Australia Ltd, Ringwood, Victoria, Australia
Penguin Books Canada Ltd, 10 Alcorn Avenue, Toronto, Ontario, Canada M4V 3B2
Penguin Books (N.Z.) Ltd, 182-190 Wairau Road, Auckland 10, New Zealand

Penguin Books Ltd, Registered Offices: Harmondsworth, Middlesex, England

First published in 1999 by Viking, a member of Penguin Putnam Books for Young Readers.
Published simultaneously in a paperback edition.

1 3 5 7 9 10 8 6 4 2

LIBRARY OF CONGRESS CATALOGING-IN-PUBLICATION DATA
Stamaty, Mark Alan.
Too many time machines / Mark Alan Stamaty.   p.   cm.
Summary: Roger uses his time machine to visit Babe Ruth and learn some of the
secrets of The Babe's success, enabling Roger's team to win the championship.
ISBN 0-670-88477-4
[1. Time travel—Fiction. 2. Baseball—Fiction.
3. Ruth, Babe, 1895-1948—Fiction. 4. Cartoons and comics.] I. Title.
PZ7.S7837To 1999 [Fic]—dc21 98-43407 CIP AC

Printed in Hong Kong
Set in OPTIVagRound

Front cover title type, New Pencil, Inc.

For Carol

Roger was bored with time machines. All his friends had them.

They spent most of their time traveling back and forth to the past and future and buying new accessories.

Roger had a time machine, too, that he'd been given for his birthday.

Baseball was Roger's life.

He was captain of his team, the Ravens. They'd won the championship two years in a row. Roger wanted to make it three.

But lately, his teammates were becoming overconfident.

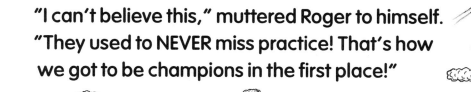

"I can't believe this," muttered Roger to himself.
"They used to NEVER miss practice! That's how
we got to be champions in the first place!"

Roger went home and sat and stewed.

What's wrong, son?

No one showed up for baseball practice. The championship game is next week and they're all off playing with their dorky time machines!

So, why don't you play with YOUR time machine?

Because I'd rather play BASEBALL!

Roger's allowance turned out to be worth a lot more
back then. He got himself a front row seat at Yankee
Stadium. When Babe Ruth came to bat, Roger could
hardly believe his eyes. In that one game,
the Babe pounded out two home runs,
higher and farther than Roger ever
dreamed was possible.

After the game, Roger ran to the clubhouse door to meet the Babe in person. There was a crowd of kids waiting to do the same.

But then a man came to the door and said the Babe had already left by a different exit. So everyone gave up and headed home.

Roger headed out to the parking lot. There was hardly anyone around. He was reading his time map to figure out the best way home when a deep voice behind him said, "Hey, kid."

Before they knew it, they were flying over Athens in 708 B.C. "Well, fry my fritters!" said the Babe. "You weren't kiddin'! This is quite a contraption you got here!"

"That looks like a stadium," said Roger. "Maybe they're playing baseball in there."

Roger landed nearby and they went inside.

Roger didn't manage to throw it very far.

Roger tried again and again. Each time he did a little better.

Hey! Good one!

You're OK, kid. You've got spunk.

Thanks, Babe. Now can we play baseball?

There's plenty of time for that. First, I gotta see what else is going on around here.

"Say, Roger, how 'bout givin' *me* a crack at drivin' this gadget?" said Babe when they got back to the time machine. "It can't be much harder than drivin' my tractor or the Model A Roadster I got back home. Just tell me what to do."

"OK," said Roger, and they climbed inside. "First, you turn the key."

"That's easy enough," said the Babe.

"Now pull the oxilation valve," said Roger, "set the time-o-meter, release the century compression activator and the zoomulsion throttle, and push those three buttons. . . . NO! NOT **THAT ONE!!**"

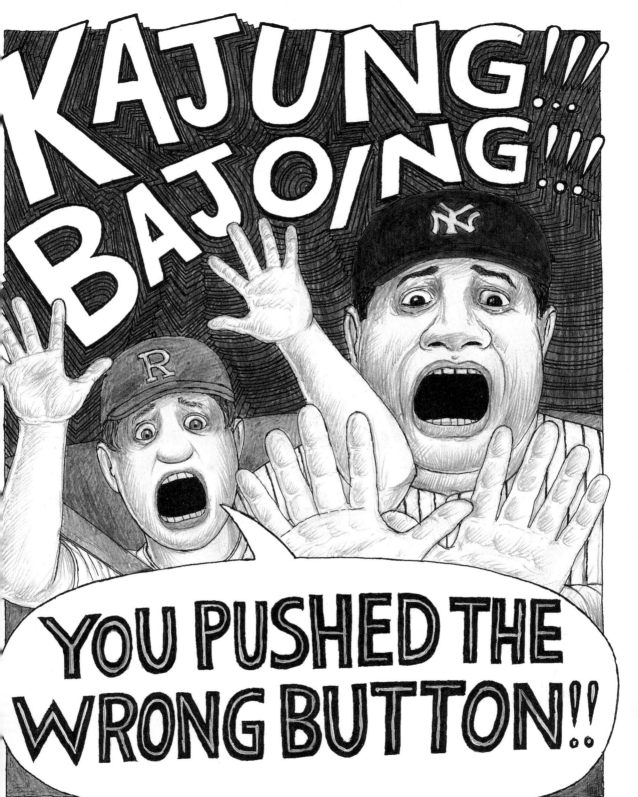

But it
was too late.
The time machine
started twirling, rumbling

sputtering, screeching, round and round.
Faster and faster it spun till all they could do
was close their eyes and hold on tight. Then they began

hearing voices of many people in many
languages, Assyrian, Babylonian, Portuguese,

When they opened their eyes, they found themselves in the midst of a very confusing scene. There were ancient Egyptians, Renaissance artists, George Washington, Queen Isabella, Elvis, and many more, all piled up in a giant Time Collision.

"What's going on here?!" said Abe Lincoln. "I've got a speech to make in Gettysburg!"

"Big deal!" said Cleopatra of ancient Egypt. "I'm late for my lunch date with Julius Caesar!"

"Everyone out of my way!" shouted Marco Polo, the explorer. "I've got to discover whole new worlds!"

"Well, I'm missing baseball practice!" said Roger finally. "But if everyone would just give my machine a push, I'll get us out of this mess, and you can all be on your way."

And
so
they
did.

On their way back, Roger and Babe were passing over the twelfth century when Roger saw several of his teammates heading in the opposite direction.

"Hey, Roger!" they shouted. "Come with us! We're going back to ancient Rome to watch a guy named Hannibal try to conquer the Romans with a bunch of armored elephants!"

"No!" said Roger. "You come with me to baseball practice!
We need to be ready for the championship game!"
    "We don't need to practice!" said his teammates.
"Nobody can beat us!"

So Roger and the Babe went back alone and practiced and practiced. Every day for the rest of the week they worked on . . .

fielding . . .

running . . .

throwing . . .

and, best of all . . .

. . . Babe taught Roger his power-hitting secrets.

...Keep your eye on the ball... step into it...

Nice one!

You're getting it!

Meanwhile, Roger's teammates discovered that ancient armies in the middle of secret invasions of enemy territory don't necessarily welcome spectators. As soon as Hannibal and his troops saw them, they attacked. And Roger's teammates barely escaped with their lives.

Things weren't so easy in the field either. It seemed like everyone on Roger's team was having trouble holding onto the ball . . .

. . . except for Roger.

In the fourth inning, the Sharks scored two runs to take the lead, 2 to 1.

But no one else on Roger's team could get a hit until the sixth inning, when Julia bunted for a single.

Then Roger came up and fouled off the first two pitches.

Then he hit the next pitch harder, higher,

and farther than anyone in Roger's league had
ever hit a baseball before. Over the fence,
over the willow trees,
and into the reservoir.
And the score was 3 to 2.

And the game was over. The Ravens had won and Roger was the hero.

That night Roger's parents invited Babe for dinner, and they had a big celebration.

The next day things got calmer.

You must feel really good about winning three championships, Roger.

I do.